The Elf and the Songbirds

A Tommy Briggs and Cindy Brown story

Other Tommy Briggs and Cindy Brown stories

The Elf and the Rainbow

The Elf and the Thunder Clouds

First Edition
Text copyright © Edwin Peat 2007
Illustrations copyright © Val Aylin 2007
Book design by Paul Aylin
Edited by Jo Aylin

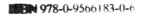 ISBN 978-0-9566183-0-6

The Elf and the Songbirds

A Tommy Briggs and Cindy Brown story

By Edwin Peat

Illustrations by Val Aylin

Once upon a time, there was a little boy called Tommy Briggs and a little girl called Cindy Brown. They lived next door to one another with their mummies and daddies. They were very good friends and used to play together after school.

Sometimes they would play in their gardens and sometimes they would go into the woods at the bottom of their gardens to watch the rabbits, squirrels and birds at play.

One day they went for a walk in the woods, their mummies telling them not to go too far.

Off they went, watching all the birds flying here, there and everywhere. After a short time Tommy told Cindy to stop and listen. Cindy could hear the birds singing. Then, all at once, she heard a small voice calling for help. They remembered what their parents had told them about going near anyone they did not know, but this was such a small voice they thought it must belong to someone very tiny. They looked around and suddenly saw a very tiny figure, no larger than Tommy's shoe, caught in a blackberry bush.

"Oh, please help me! I am stuck fast in this bush and I can't get out."

Tommy and Cindy looked at each other, for this tiny figure was dressed all in green.

"Who are you?" asked Tommy,

"I am the Elf of Good Deeds," the tiny figure replied. "Please help me."

Very carefully Tommy and Cindy helped the elf out of the brambles. "Oh, thank you so much," said the elf. "Now, how can I repay you?"

"We don't need repaying," said Cindy.

"But I must do something to repay your kindness," said the elf and, before you could say abracadabra, he had waved a magic wand and both Tommy and Cindy became as small as the elf. Well, they were both very frightened.

"Don't be afraid," said the elf. "I will make you your proper size again when I have shown you something very special. Just follow me!"

Off the elf went with Tommy and Cindy close behind him. Do you know where they went? The elf jumped straight down a rabbit hole and Tommy and Cindy followed him. Soon they came to a door on which the elf knocked and they all went in. Mr and Mrs Rabbit were there, sitting at the table, just having lunch. The elf said how sorry he was to disturb them and then went through another door.

Here bright lights were shining and Tommy and Cindy could hear beautiful bird voices.

A little further down the passage they came to yet another door, from behind which the bird voices seemed to come. When the elf opened the door, the noise was deafening, for there were lots of birds all talking at once. Standing in front of them was a tall bird with spectacles on the end of his beak. He had a stick under his wing and banged on the table for silence.

"Silence!" he cried. "Silence!" All the birds became very quiet.

"Mr Crow, I do not think your voice is really for singing. It is only for shouting. Go outside and shout at people! Frighten them with your noise! You, Mr and Mrs. Magpie, go outside because you do nothing but chatter! Go and chatter amongst yourselves and leave the song-birds to practise their chorus."

"Now that the noisy ones have gone," said the learned-looking bird, "We will continue."

All the birds stood up straight, the blackbirds, the thrushes and all the other song-birds.

"Now," said the learned bird, "Let us try again." The sound was wonderful. Tommy and Cindy were amazed. They had never heard such beautiful singing.

"Well," said the elf, "That was a surprise for you. Come along now. It is time you were going home. I must ask you not to say a word about your adventure to anyone. Promise?" Tommy and Cindy promised that this would be their secret.

Off they went down a long passage with lots of doors leading from it. "I wonder what is behind those doors?" thought Tommy.

Soon they saw daylight and, pop! Out they came from a rabbit hole, just by the one they had slid down.

"It is time to say goodbye," said the elf and, with a wave of his wand, Tommy and Cindy became their normal size. By now it was time to go home for tea, so off they skipped, remembering not to tell anyone their secret.

I wonder what adventure Tommy and Cindy will have next.